SAM DOWLING

Is a Dublin-born playwright. He has written and produced nearly thirty plays or small-cast versions of classics for Praxis Theatre Laboratory. His subject-matter has ranged from Irish history through the lives of writers and artists to re-working of themes from the Greek myths. His play about the Brontës (co-written with Andrea Bird) has had three productions in Tokyo.

For more detail see listing in playwrights' database at www.doollee.com

PRAXIS THEATRE LABORATORY is an experimental theatre which seeks its direction from the actors' response to the work. No-one takes on a separate role as director. We particularly value images conjured in rehearsal, and intuitive and emotional rather than intellectual or technical evaluation. We try to fix as little as possible and each performance retains an element of improvisation.

Founded by Sam Dowling as the in-house company at The Tabard in West London from 1984, in 1990 we left to pursue more experimental goals. We opened a small theatre space in County Roscommon, Ireland in 1999 and have toured UK, USA, Ireland, Belgium, Netherlands, Ukraine and Poland.

ALLEGIANCE was first performed at The Tabard Theatre, Turnham Green in West London on 1st June 1989, with this cast:

MAY .... Ann Haydn

LUKE ....Nick Ellsworth

TOM ....Jeffrey Harmer

MAURA..Celia Nelson

Designed by Paul Dowling

IRISH PLAYS AND OTHERS BY SAM DOWLING
IN PRINT AT WWW.LULU.COM OR IN THE PIPELINE

RIVERMAN [Walter Greaves, naïf painter, rise and fall.]
CAULDRON OF BRONTËS [Genius siblings.]
A SEASON IN HELL [Wild poets Rimbaud and Verlaine.]
MOUNTAIN [Life-changing encounters]
RENEWAL [Site-specific version of MOUNTAIN]
TROJAN WOMEN
BIRTH OF THE BEAST [Northern Ireland.]
BIG FELLA! [Michael Collins]
ALLEGIANCE [IRA in London.]
ANTIGONE
THE FLAME AND THE STONE [Yeats and Maud Gonne.]
VIRGIN OF NOTTING HILL [Sexual problems.]
ORESTEIAN TRILOGY
LOVELOST [Abuse]
RED COUNTESS GREEN CROW [Markievicz and O'Casey]
HA! HA! HA! [Improvisations on Coward and Shakespeare.]
CHARTISTS RISING [London 1848]

AND SMALL-CAST VERSIONS OF THESE CLASSICS;

THE CENCI
IMPORTANCE OF BEING EARNEST
CHERRY ORCHARD
THREE SISTERS
HEDDA GABLER
WHEN WE DEAD AWAKEN
HAMLET
MACBETH
ANTONY AND CLEOPATRA
THE TEMPEST

IRISH PLAYS AND OTHERS Vol. 15

ALLEGIANCE

by

Sam Dowling [writing as "Sean O' Hare"]

1988

E-mail praxis.lab@ntlworld.com

Published by Lulu 2008

www.lulu.com

ISBN 978-1-4092-0081-9

ALLEGIANCE

CHARACTERS

MAY..........................Fortyish. Irish but speaks Standard English.

TOM..........................Her son. Early twenties. Same accent.

MAURA.....................His sister. A couple of years younger.
Irish accent.

LUKE.........................Early forties. English.

SETTING. The play is set in present-day London: MAY's flat is in a gentrified street near Notting Hill.

ACT ONE

[The denuded living room of May's flat. A 78rpm record of THESE FOOLISH THINGS is playing on an antique gramophone, which sits atop a very modern TV.
MAY, expensively dressed, makes up before a piece of broken mirror.
TOM looks about for somewhere to work on his research.]

TOM — I mean, it's the third time in seven years I've come home to find....
May, the bailiffs carrying the dining table... I met them.... I had the image of your coffin going down the stairs....

MAY — Lord! That evokes a whole generation!

TOM — Bailiffs evoke nothing in me but cold horror!

MAY — The song

TOM — Nothing

[TOM sits on the floor to work.]

MAY — Philistine

TOM — I'm trying to work.........
Observe my stern realism in the midst of chaos!

MAY — Not chaotic: it's.... uncluttered. I like it. Anyway, you're no realist: a died-in-the-wool romantic. How could you be anything else, with me for a .... and your unfortunate father over there these past twenty years trying to die to free Ireland...

TOM — Bill is more interested in free Guinness that a free Ireland...

MAY — ...... At forty you'll be a sentimentalist like me

TOM — The past is a clean slate as far as......

MAY — Wait till you've had a past before you say that

TOM — I'd resent that, madam, if I hadn't forgotten my murky youth

MAY — I had a wonderful childhood... waited on hand and foot, like Royalty

TOM — Grandpa? Hmmm
Grandpa had no love in him.....Mad as a March hare

MAY — He loved me

TOM — He loved himself
None of our family know how to love...really love

MAY — Thank you, kind sir

[TOM is winding the gramophone. He will start to turn the record over.]

TOM Because we're insatiable

MAY Just once more, TOM

[TOM will start to play the same side again.]

TOM Having children should be licensed... like pilots

MAY Is that needle all right?

TOM ....
You didn't want me

MAY That doesn't stop me loving you

TOM You should have got an ab.....

[MAY reaches out her arms to him.]

MAY Dance!

[MAY sings along with the recorded vocalist.]
"A cigarette that bears the lipstick traces..."

TOM Aw May, I can't

MAY *"An airline ticket to romantic places..."*
Come!

[MAY and TOM dance close together.]

"As if my heart had wings
These foolish things remind me of you...."

You're a lovely dancer: you get that from me. Bill couldn't put one foot in front of the other.

………………………………

You're going stiff

[TOM breaks away]

Oh just like your father. No give

[MAY dances on her own, singing with the record. TOM tries to read, but can't.]

"A wind of March that made my heart a dancer,
A telephone that rings but who's to answer..."
I hate dancing on my own; it's indecent

TOM You frightened me...

MAY Don't be silly

TOM You and Bill......
The hammer and the anvil...

MAY Swift and Goldsmith

………………………

Bill was definitely 'hammer'.... I'm 'anvil'

……………………

You're a bit of a mixture. I like that: it makes you more interesting

TOM In England, I've been really passive

MAY The writing, the research: that's not passive

TOM I'm so bloody happy just doing it!

Part of it is having got you out of Bill's clutches

MAY — I could feel.... what would you call it? a palpable violence in the room with the two of you. I knew it was a choice between you and him

TOM — Luke and him

MAY — No.....

TOM — I hate everything my father stood for

MAY — .... You

TOM — It's unnatural

MAY — Having my own flesh and blood reincarnated in a man: that brought... brings me a sense of utter completeness. No ordinary man ever gave me that

TOM — You think I'm safe. A man who doesn't make sexual demands on you

MAY — I feel... demands. But you don't make me afraid because you're that mixture

TOM — Your own reflection...

MAY — Narcissus!

TOM — May..... when we were dancing.....I had to stop

....

I felt engulfed...........losing control: like a child

MAY

Sometimes I go on drinking and drinking, so I'll lose control........ awareness. It doesn't work. I just throw it all up. My mind won't befuddle.......The Irish curse

....

....

That feeling of being swallowed up.......... You know you made extraordinary demands on me as a child?

TOM

I'll pay you back.
I'll look after you if you grow old before me: which looks increasingly unlikely

MAY

For three, nearly four years, you wouldn't let me out of your sight. If I walked into the other room you'd have hysterics

TOM

I didn't know there was another room: I thought the world was a box. When you went out I was convinced you'd fallen into a Black Hole....

MAY

Couldn't even go to the toilet on my own till...till I got you off to play-school, really. It took away all... autonomy

TOM

If I was my mother, I'd run away

MAY

I did. Not from you
Did I ever tell you how I met Luke?

TOM

It's about time you let him move in permanently: at least it'd put a stop to... this sort of thing.

MAY

Poor Papa thought I was cracking up under Bill's Corporate State regime, which I was, so he made me an appointment with this

Harley Street Specialist .... Bought me my ticket, hotel and everything and put me on the boat at Dun Laoghaire himself in case the Storm Troopers decided to interfere. I was barely out of sight of the Dublin Mountains when I knew it wasn't a psychiatrist I needed. First thing I did in London was I went out and spent half the doctor's fees on a beautiful new dress in Oxford Street. I phoned him, this Consultant... I mean he was one of the top men in London. I told him there wasn't a thing wrong with me that a good day at the Races wouldn't cure and that's what I was going to do with the other half of his fees. Well, I thought he'd die laughing at the other end of the phone! He said for two pins he'd close shop and come with me!

It was a Friday, so the racing was at Goodwood. I met Luke on the train from Victoria, me as usual traveling First on a Third Class Ticket: he rescued me from a ticket inspector with some interminable story.... He was so handsome and always laughing. No one could resist him and that's how I met him

Anyway, the upshot was that Papa couldn't believe the improvement in my condition after just one visit to his psychiatrist friend: he swore by him till the day he died! Naturally, one visit led to another.... Dublin and Bill!

TOM

There are at least four couples I know, who can't wait to get married: hurling themselves at it like so many Gaderine swine. What the hell is it? I mean, not one of their parents is even remotely happy...

MAY

I didn't even think about marriage: I wanted a wedding. A white wedding and my picture in Social & Personal! Marriage was sprung on me as some sort of macabre practical joke, shortly after the sherry trifle

TOM

No coffee?

MAY

Bill didn't want coffee.
……………………… We went upstairs to change for going away…………………… Your father………… ravished me, I suppose you'd call it, while I was still in my virginal white taffeta……….
What had emerged was a distinct conflict of interests

TOM

He was your husband

MAY

I screamed a bit. Bill held his hand over my mouth………….
There was blood everywhere. I don't think I've seen so much blood. He was wearing this white dress suit. I don't know if it was ………….. my virginity or menstruation or what. Both probably: I don't know.
My beautiful dress and veil………. I stuffed them down the toilet

TOM

They wouldn't go down the toilet

MAY

That's what I did with them…. It was just another mess.
I left a five-pound note for the cleaner

TOM

………………………
………………………

If I ever lose my virginity, I'll insist on it being properly supervised.....

MAY Don't tell me you're still..........

TOM The family lawyer........ the faithful family physician in solemn attendance........

MAY Ha! You're having me on!

TOM My experience was quite beautiful really... Our first Summer in London..... that flat over the junk shop in Goldhawk Road

MAY Don't remind me!

TOM Well, I liked it.
You and Luke were off gallivanting for the weekend....

MAY Brittany. We used to walk the coastline from pub to pub, looking for the farms Gauguin painted

TOM Anyway, you were barely out of sight when.... You remember the wee Scottish girl across the landing? She came in to borrow a cup of milk or something..........

MAY Oh she was gorgeous! Annie

TOM I hadn't a chance! Her boyfriend was moving in with her permanently the following week and she just set up some kind of fling for herself. Sunday morning in that pub by the river........ The Ship.......
I asked her to marry me. She laughed. She wouldn't say anything: just laughed and ran off down the lane and back to the flat. I

lost a lot of weight and sleep over wee Annie

MAY — So much for your Gaderine swine!

TOM — I tried to join them: they wouldn't have me. It's all sour grapes

MAY — We live on phantasy or memories. Either way we make our own paradise

TOM — That's really bad politics: live in the here and now. Real situations, real people

MAY — My friends are real. Who ever had a better friend than Luke? I weave around him a chrysalis of wonderful romance... old songs and memories of all the warmth and goodness I ever knew

TOM — I can hear poor Marx turning in his grave. You can't just build a cocoon around your lives: there are problems to be solved. Here....

MAY — We seem to survive

TOM — I got no........ guidance from you

MAY — I trust you

TOM — Even as a child

MAY — You were always too sensible if anything

TOM — And what about Maura: she is your only daughter

MAY Maura knows I'd love to have her here. It was her decision

TOM She was about fourteen

MAY She must be a good influence on Bill. She comes over... quite often

TOM Bill must be a bad influence on her

MAY I trust her

TOM Maybe I should go back and keep an eye on her

MAY ....

I don't want to think about Bill! Ever. If he'd pay me by Banker's Order I might forget him completely. He won't, of course. The monthly cheque gives him an illusion of........ fecundity

TOM Please stop taking anything from him

MAY .... ?

I like being dependent.

....

Anyway, he has to pay retribution for messing up my life. He was old enough to know better. I was only an infant. I was hardly nineteen when you arrived

TOM You could have had an abortion

MAY In Ireland? And it was a mortal sin. It probably still is, God help them, which he doesn't. Bill was a great Catholic...... he used to make me cover the bruises on my face with the old Max Factor so we wouldn't miss Mass on Sunday morning. Poor Bill......

[MAY sings with the gramophone.]

"...... *These foolish things remind me of you.....*"

[TOM winds the machine.]

Don't overwind it

TOM ....
What was I like...... as a kid?

MAY (Kindly) The ugliest child I ever set eyes on, poor wee mite.............

[TOM turns his back on her.]

But I loved you.
I remember my sister saying to me: "May", she said, "how can you call a child 'ugly' that has eyes like that?"

TOM Eyes

MAY You know I love you: you and Maura.
You're all I have really................
....
Dance!

[TOM ignores the invitation: he is leafing through a sheaf of May's bills.]

TOM — It's humiliating: the bailiffs hauling the furniture out from under you every other year!

MAY — You never really wanted for anything

TOM — God

....

Why don't you get a job?

[MAY makes a helpless gesture.]

I don't begrudge you the few pounds I give you

MAY — You're very good to me: every one of you

TOM — So much talent. You're a handsome, intelligent young woman. Why don't you find a career for yourself?

MAY — I hear Luke! What time is it? Aw, they took Papa's clock! Isn't that shameful!

TOM — Of course it's shameful

MAY — Luke will get it back for me............

[MAY straightens her clothes and will go to the comforting embrace of LUKE when he lets himself in. LUKE is big; a sporting type, a year or two older than MAY and a very successful Q.C.]

MAY — Oh Luke!

LUKE — Hello May love! Lord! Spring cleaning time again, is it? Hello Tom

TOM	Hi Luke
MAY	They walked in and took everything
LUKE	And you just stood there gawping at them, Tom?
TOM	I'm only in half an hour......
MAY	He came back from Leeds specially
LUKE	All you had to do was say the stuff was all mine for godsakes! I mean, it is, in a way....
MAY	I can't bluff: you know that. Tom saved Papa's gramophone. "That's mine!" he says, quick as anything. The man never even questioned it. Then he said the TV was rented............
LUKE	May, you said you'd paid all those bills
MAY	Please don't start on me, Luke
	[LUKE sighs and moves towards the TV.]
LUKE	Anyone mind if I get the Market Prices? Things were a bit shaky this morning
TOM	The electricity is cut off
LUKE	Aw May! .... How much are we talking about?
MAY	Four hundred

LUKE They couldn't clear you out for four hund.....

TOM Four hundred is the electricity ......

LUKE WHAT?.......... Oh never mind. How much is it altogether, May?

MAY I don't know

LUKE A thousand?

MAY I suppose so

LUKE Two?

MAY Hardly

TOM More like twelve

MAY It couldn't be twelve

TOM It's out of my league. I could throw in a couple of hundred, but...

LUKE Did they get the mink?

MAY Good lord!

[MAY rushes from the room. LUKE reaches out for the bills. TOM checks the phone.]

LUKE Is this the lot?

TOM Phone still connected. Did you see a bill in the hall?

LUKE

Probably. You know what May's like about bills: 'if you don't open them, they may go away.'

TOM

I'll have a look.

[Exit TOM. MAY is heard laughing a little hysterically before she re-enters wearing a fine mink.]

MAY

I hung it out of the toilet window when I heard them at the door: it's the only thing I could think of.
Isn't it beautiful?

LUKE

What about the pearls?

[MAY pats her crotch.]

May!

....

Ha, ha, ha! Well, things could be worse as the man said when he swallowed the tenner. 'At least we know where the next meal is coming from!' Ha ha ha ha...

[LUKE is sorting through the bills.]

LUKE continues

Barclays... Midland... Lloyds... Barclays Kensington... Barclays Piccadilly... How many banks are you with, May?

MAY

..........................?

LUKE

The Bank of where............!?

MAY That's the nice Arab gentleman we met at Ascot. You should never have given me this beautiful mink, Luke... it's a... a license to print money. I just walk into any bank I'm passing and get an overdraft.

LUKE Well, I'm going to revoke your license if you don't behave yourself.
I'll see what I can do with...
May, I can only pull a stroke like this once.
You'll have t....

MAY You're so good to me!

[MAY hugs and kisses him. LUKE responds hungrily, but MAY demurs and extricates himself affectionately.]

MAY Easy does it

LUKE You're not fair with me, May. I need a lot of.... affection

[MAY hugs him safely.]

MAY And you get it, you cuddly big lump

LUKE We haven't made love for a week

MAY I wasn't well

LUKE Can I stay the night?

MAY Look at the place!

LUKE Did they leave the bed?

MAY I think so

LUKE Come on!

MAY Tom will be back in......

LUKE Go in: I'll take care of Tom

MAY We'll make love later, Luke: I promise. I'm ravenous!

LUKE You're not going to get drunk just because you have to make love with me, May? It makes me feel a real shit

MAY I promise

[Enter TOM.]

Let's go out and have a really scrumptious meal somewhere!

TOM Not me: honest! I've been neglecting my love-life. Two weeks research in Leeds is unbearably stimulating for the old libido...

LUKE Still on the Luddites, are you?

TOM I started off, trying to record the assimilation into the English working class, of three desperately poor Irish immigrant families: they had settled in a ghetto in Leeds during the Napoleonic Wars...

LUKE My father always said we had Irish blood, way back somewhere on his mother's side

TOM Politically, I was really disappointed. Two of my families were incredibly mobile... they went up through the class system like a dose of salts. By the early nineteen hundreds they were dyed-in-the-wool

English High Tories: they'd changed their name, religion, class... allegiances right across the board, even nationality

MAY That's the only way to get on

TOM Who wants to get on?
I'm now working the other way round. I'm taking three radical families with possible Irish origins, Trade Unionists, and I'm tracing them back to see what factors influenced their very different development.....

LUKE This will be a novel, will it?

TOM I hope so

MAY Come with us, Tom

TOM Honestly, I....

LUKE You'd be more than welcome

TOM I have to make a few calls

MAY I like that girl whatsername.... From Hampstead

TOM She's top of my list

MAY Excuse me fellas while I....

[MAY turns away to fish a string of pearls from her pants.]

Luke, be a darling, will you....?

[LUKE fixes the clasp of the pearls. He kisses the side of her neck.]

Mmmm Thank you

[MAY moves out of reach.]

How do I grab you?

LUKE — Like.... Dinner at the Ritz

MAY — We have to economise. Claridges

LUKE — The Ritz. I just couldn't go wrong all day

MAY — Luke's defending in this big share scandal thing... very prestigious

LUKE — I was talking about the gee-gees. Did you back those horses at Newmarket?

MAY — I can't gamble... even with Luke's money

LUKE — There was no gamble, May. The first race was a moral certainty at five to four

Tom — Neither can I

LUKE — Michael won at least a grand on it

TOM — ....?

MAY — Haverton. Secretary of State for what is it, Luke? Police and all that kind of thing

LUKE — Home Affairs

MAY He's yummy

LUKE Well, he's a real human being. He's more of a true radical than all your Labour Party hacks put together, Tom

MAY He wants Luke to stand in the next election

LUKE And I want him to get out of politics... he's too honest and he's too intelligent for that game

MAY And so are you

TOM The Conservatives is it?

LUKE I've no intention of getting into that can of worms... the Law is bad enough. But if I did... yes, I'd join the Conservatives. The Conservatives represent power and ownership in this country: so that's where real change can be generated

TOM All the change that lot generate goes into their trousers' pockets

LUKE Ha ha ha ha!
No. Most of them are good decent people...
Well, maybe not 'good'... Ha ha ha!

TOM And maybe not 'decent'? Ha ha ha!

LUKE But definitely 'people'! No? Ha ha ha!

[The doorbell rings]

TOM I'll get it

MAY Lord! They're back for the coat!

[MAY runs for the other door with the coat. She pauses as we hear animated VOICES OFF. Enter MAURA and TOM with arms around each other. MAURA has a travelling bag. MAY immediately recovers her aplomb and goes elegantly towards MAURA's warm embrace.]

MAURA May! I should have written or...

MAY Maura! Oh it's lovely to see you!

MAURA Jaysus May, where did the coat come out of?

MAY You remember Luke. Maura? You look... I'll make you a cup of tea

TOM My twist

[Exit Tom.]

MAURA Oh Luke!

[MAURA kisses LUKE full on the mouth and growls her pleasure.]

MAURA Grrr! I don't know how you do it , May... at your age! Ha ha ha! I'm only havin you on: more power to your elbow, the pair of you! Plenty of winners these days, Luke?

LUKE I gave four winners to your mother today at Newmarket, and she wouldn't even put a pound on them. Five to four, two to one and two even money winners. Michael Haverton laid eight hundred on the first race and played with the bookies' money all day

MAURA Haverton? The Michael Haverton?

MAY He wants Luke to stand

MAURA He must have won what? About six grand. Any tips like that for tomorrow, Luke?

LUKE I won't know till about... My man doesn't open his mouth till he has his own bets down

MAURA I'll give you a fiver to bet for me....

LUKE No. I never lay other people's bets... it's bad luck for me. Phone me at the Savoy Grill say one fifteen to one thirty and I'll make your fortune for you

MAURA A few pounds is my limit

LUKE Quite right too

MAY Those bookies' shops give me the creeps

MAURA May, have you no furniture?

MAY Oh don't ask me about it, Maura. It's a long story

[Enter TOM, with tea things.]

TOM It's Save-The-Bailiffs Week again

MAURA	May!
MAY	I don't want to talk about anything unpleasant. We're making a fresh start
LUKE	Did they leave the cooker and...?
TOM	Cooker and beds. They wouldn't want to deprive the needy of the wherewithal to either start another family or put an end to the entire thing!
LUKE	May's cooking isn't all that lethal! Ha ha ha ha!
TOM	We live in a caring society here, Maura
LUKE	Well yes, we do really
TOM	Cradle to the gas oven! Your future is safe with us...
LUKE	No danger of anyone here sticking their head in the gas oven, Tom. That's what I like about May's family: full of the old *joie de vivre eh?*
TOM	*Moi ?* Full of *joie ?*
LUKE	You're a wee bit too serious at times, Tom...
MAY	He works too hard
LUKE	...But the women in the family are... perfect! Eh. Maura?

[LUKE hugs MAURA, who responds more enthusiastically than he expects. MAY is busy with the tea.]

TOM — I see this country heading back to the days of the Poor Laws if the Conservatives get....

LUKE — Poppycock. They made the economy as tight as a drum...

MAURA — I wouldn't like to see you in politics, Luke

LUKE — Everything is what you make it

MAURA — No, it's what it makes you....
Please!

LUKE — Now who's getting serious? Politics here isn't like Ulster, Maura. Or Dublin. I never liked the look of that Taoiseach fellow

MAURA — Politicians become kind of caricatures...

MAY — I know Luke: nothing would change him. My only fear would be he'd have no privacy. I don't think you could take that.

TOM — I should very much like to see you as a judge rather than a cabinet minister...

MAURA — Hey! What happened to your accents?

TOM — Pardon?

MAURA — I knew there was something funny about you two

MAY	Darling...
Maura	"Dawling!" Aw, please May
TOM	The last time you were over...
MAURA	"Lawst!" Cut it out, Tom, for Chisake: You're talking like a bloody Englishman. Sorry Luke, it's so false when they...
TOM	I'm speaking English
MAURA	Why can't you speak the way you always spoke?
TOM	I really don't know what you m...
MAURA	Fucking well you know what I mean: you spoke like me all your fucking life
TOM	You spoke beautifully when we all lived together. It really doesn't suit you: you have a degree in English. Your vocabulary surely extends beyond the single and rather tedious expletive, 'fucking'. It does little credit to your education and imagination...
MAURA	Bollocks!
MAY	He's right. It doesn't suit you, Maura
MAURA	You're both making a big mistake. You'll never be English just by aping their accent...
LUKE	Their speech is natural and distinctive. I love the richness of their vocabulary and imagery. It's not at all English

TOM We've been here seven years

MAURA If you're not Irish, you're nothing. Nothing!

TOM I'm not sure I can accept adjectives like 'Irish' or 'English' any more.......
You know the one about the out-of-work actor who crawls, starving, to answer a phone-call from a Hollywood producer. "Are you Jewish?" the producer finally asks him, just as he appeared to be about to offer him this fantastic part. There's a silence, then the actor answers. "Am I Jewish?.....Not necessarily...."

[MAY and LUKE are amused.]

MAURA Are you coming back?

TOM I shouldn't think so

MAURA Everything is a game for you, Tom
Are you coming back, May?

MAY No love: I couldn't breathe there

MAURA And neither of you gives a shit what happens to your country

MAY I have two countries. The man I love is here

TOM I have no country

[Phone rings. MAY answers it.]

MAY 4827!

MAURA — You can't talk your way out of your nationality

MAY — Luke!

[LUKE goes to the phone.]

TOM — What I have succeeded in doing is thinking myself out of my Nationalism

LUKE — Tom. Tom! Maura... Cool it a minute, will you!

[TOM and MAURA continue to argue in a whisper. TOM will storm out, leaving MAURA staring at LUKE. MAY is ready to leave for the Ritz.]

LUKE — Hello! Hello Michael: how are you old son? .... Ha ha ha! I'm delighted..... No no no no. A pleasure! You can buy me lunch some day........ Tomorrow? Why not!....... Sure. That would be really nice..... The usual........... One fifteen would be perfect, Michael............. The Grill. Look forward to seeing you.................................
Ha ha ha ha I'll try! Ha ha ha...................

MAY — I'll just faint if I don't eat

LUKE — Have you eaten, Maura?

MAURA — Aw no, I won't be a gooseberry! You could drop me near a tube though....

LUKE — You're coming with us

MAY Oh do, Maura: Luke is taking us to the Ritz!

MAURA I couldn't go to the Ritz like this!

MAY Wear the mink

MAURA I...

[MAY puts the mink on MAURA.]

I couldn't

[MAY hugs LUKE.]

MAY [Sings.] *I've got my love to keep me warm....*

LUKE Stunning!

MAURA Are you sure, May?

LUKE And now we're going to buy you the meal of your life: We're celebrating! What's this we're celebrating, May?

MAY Eh..... A new beginning!

....

I think I'd like the whole place in a kind if palest of pale pinky white....

LUKE Don't tell me on an empty stomach! Ha ha ha ha ......

[MAURA is trying to look at herself in the broken mirror.]

MAURA You sure I won't be in the way?

LUKE A beautiful young woman is never in the way, Maura

MAY Oh excuse me! Am I in the way?

LUKE I said ' a beautiful young woman in never in the way'

MAY Sorry, I didn't hear you

[Exeunt.
MAURA returns and calls after them.]

MAURA I'll just run to the loo! See you in the car...

[MAURA goes quickly to the phone and dials. She speaks urgently during SLOW BLACKOUT.]

George? Things are moving very fast. You're changing trains: savez? A snip. Centre city. But I need to see you tonight......... Listen! The Ritz........ in the foyer in exactly one hour. That's right. We're going to meet by accident: I'll be on my way to the loo or something.... The Ritz Hotel... it's the poshest fucking hotel in the world.... Opposite Green Park Tube Station... that's it.... And you'd better put on a decent suit... try to look like a doctor or something.... Of course you'll have to wear a fucking tie! Yes....... Exactly one hour from now........ Slán.

[The evening passes.]

[Enter MAURA, MAY and LUKE, in various stages of inebriation.

MAURA and LUKE are supporting MAY, who is quite drunk. They will leave her swaying in centre of room while they go about placing and lighting candles.]

MAURA Who needs electricity?

MAY I need music......

MAURA I'll do it

[MAURA will play a record on the gramophone.]

LUKE The only reason I eat at the Ritz is so I can nick their candles....

MAURA That old doll at the next table actually lives there, or so she says

MAY I'd live there if I had the money: it's very homely

....

Where's the furniture?

LUKE Better get you into bed, May

MAY Right. We'll have one little drink and then we'll get you into bed, May

LUKE I couldn't

MAURA Nothing for me

MAY If we won't drink, we'll dance

[MAY dances a step or two and falls.]

MAY — Where's the furniture? I fell over the couch cos it's not there....

MAURA — Up, May

[MAURA will help her up.]

LUKE — The furniture is gone. The bailiffs took it

MAY — I did the whole place out about an hour ago.... The pinkiest of paley white.... Now it's gone as you so rightly remark, Luke.... 'Scuse me.....

[MAY heads towards the bathroom. MAURA follows to the door.]

MAURA — She's all right, I think

LUKE — You know why that is: why she's pissed out if her loaf?

MAURA — She was having a ball

LUKE — I love your mother deeply

MAURA — You're a lucky pair

LUKE — We have a problem

MAURA — I'll help get some furniture....

LUKE — That's.....
You know why she's like this tonight?

MAURA	Same reason as us
LUKE	We have a nice meal.... Wine... you're not drunk....
MAURA	I am
LUKE	... I'm not dunk... drunk.... But May's dunk
MAURA	I'm dunk
LUKE	This is serious, Maura. She can't face making love with me less she's sloshed out of her mind....
MAURA	She thinks the world of you
LUKE	I'm telling you: I love her..... A man needs a sexual life
MAURA	A woman needs a sexual life
LUKE	Not May
MAURA	Of course she does....
LUKE	Simple as that. Hates me to ev.... She's a warm, sexually attractive woman th.... Do you think I'm revolting?
MAURA	You're a handsome, intelligent, successful....
LUKE	Would you want to make love with me?
MAURA	If you were my man, yes I would
LUKE	I don't know whether to talk about you and me or May and me

MAURA I have my own man

LUKE Tell me

MAURA I'd prefer talk about you and May

LUKE What's his name?

MAURA ……………………
George

LUKE English

MAURA Irish. It's a kind of pet name

LUKE Bloody strange pet name. 'George'
……………………
Mind if I ask you a very personal question?

MAURA Yes.
Go on

LUKE Do you… have you this same kind of problem as May… with your man?

MAURA No

LUKE I find you….. I mean, I was wondering was I particularly attracted to women with…. difficulties

MAURA My only difficulty is getting enough of it: ha ha ha ha….

LUKE Gawd!

MAURA I'm joking, Luke. I have quite an ordinary sexual appetite which is reasonably well….

very well satisfied in my relationship with 'George'

LUKE

I mean, not because it's fashionable: I really want just one stable relationship. Nobody has ever made my life so happy as May has done, apart from....

[Enter MAY: shaky.]

MAY

How much was the bill tonight, Luke?

LUKE

Are you feeling better?

MAY

I've just flushed about forty quid's worth of *haute cuisine* down the toilet

LUKE

You promised you wouldn't do this to me

MAY

It was all so.......... perfect............
I love you very much........ Luke and Maura and Tom: you're all I've got really......... Are you coming?

[MAY reaches out her hand to LUKE. She turns her back as LUKE tries to kiss MAURA quite sexually. MAURA sends him packing, kindly.]

LUKE

Good night, Maura

MAURA

Off with the pair of you, now! See you in the morning

[MAURA re-starts the record on the gramophone. Exeunt MAY and LUKE to bedroom. MAURA moves slowly to the telephone and dials.]

MAURA

George? .... You looked fine. You checked out our friend? ....
My mother's.................... yes........................
Then you get offside, preferably on the tube..
Have a nice holiday. And no John Wayne stuff...Slán .

[The music rises to fill the theatre. MAURA extinguishes the candles in SLOW BLACKOUT.

The song takes us through the night and to early next afternoon.]

RECORDING

A piano tinkling in the next apartment
Those stumbling words that told you what my heart meant
Oh how the ghost of you clings
These foolish things remind me of you

[The phone rings unanswered.]

A wind of March that made my heart a dancer
A telephone that rings but who's to answer
A fairground's painted swings
These foolish things remind me of you...

[PHONE and MUSIC cease as MAY and MAURA enter in high spirits. POLICE SIREN outside.]

MAURA

The phone was ringing

MAY

You see what I meant: the couch down along there a chair about here.... I must get some decent pictures.........................
Luke has given me a *carte blanche*: isn't he a treasure?

[MAURA goes to window.]

MAURA

Why don't you marry him? There's a police car outside

MAY

I couldn't be bothered. Anyway, your father told me he wouldn't recognise a divorce. I don't want a fuss. Is he still the ardent Catholic and all that?

MAURA

He didn't eat for a week when he discovered I was on the pill......................
It's gone

MAY

Bill has the mind of a troglodyte

MAURA

Only as far as religion goes

MAY

And women

[A rising but muffled HUBUB within the building.]

MAURA

A bit

MAY

And politics

MAURA

There's nothing wrong with his politics..........a wee bit short on the socialist side, but basically sound

MAY

Don't let him push you into anything, love

MAURA Nobody pushes this kid into anything, May. Anyway, I take my philosophy and my politics straight from my beautiful featherbrained mother!

[MAURA and MAY alarmed as the HUBUB is heard loudly and briefly. Hall door of flat bangs shut. Door of living room bursts open to reveal LUKE swaying and bloodstained, head swathed in bandages. MAURA almost swoons. MAY rushes to LUKE.]

MAY Luke!

LUKE WHY DIDN'T YOU ANSWER THE PHONE?

MAY What is it, Luke? What happened/

MAURA I'll get a doctor

[MAURA lifts the phone.]

LUKE I've been bloody shot! Why didn't you answer the phone? I thought you were all bloody murdered! Forget it, Maura: I've seen a doctor.... It's too late for a doctor

MAY Luke!

LUKE They've killed Michael

MAY Michael? Michael Haverton? Where? Who?

LUKE — I don't know..... the bloody IRA or some other gang of lunatics: what does it matter who killed him? He's dead! He's bloody dead!

MAY — Are you hurt.... Are you all right, love?

LUKE — I'm sorry..... yes, I'm all right: I've seen a doctor

MAURA — The police?

MAY — Your suit! You're soaked in.... it's blood! Come..... I'll get a bath r.....

LUKE — A bath! What good's a bath? I'm soaked in the blood of my best friend....

MAY — You'll have to change

LUKE — They shot us from right there..... like it was all in slow motion.... These two blokes walked over to Michael and.... To us.... They had revolvers or something and they just started shooting him.... He was eating his lunch.... He fell across my lap and they kept shooting at us....

MAY — Animals!

LUKE — The waiter...... Christ! ...... the waiter scraped his brains,,,,, off...... his brains off my...... I'm going to be sick again......

[MAURA and MAY help him across the room. He shakes them off.]

PIGS! IRISH PIGS! Sorry, May, love, I'm sorry....

MAURA — We have no monopoly on murder, Luke

[LUKE turns to the audience.]

LUKE — BLOODY MURDERING IRISH PIGS!

MAURA — FOR GOD'S SAKE, LUKE.... YOU'VE BEEN TRYING TO WIPE US OUT FOR EIGHT HUNDRED YEARS!

LUKE — PIGS! PIGS!

[LUKE stumbles out to get sick.]

MUSIC.

MAY and MAURA look at their bloodstained hands as we go into SLOW BLACKOUT.]

RECORDING — *A cigarette that bears the lipstick traces*
An airline ticket to romantic places
As if my heart had wings
These foolish things remind me of you...

END OF ACT ONE

ACT TWO

[The same. A day or two later. Signs of re-furnishing going on. MAY's father's CLOCK is back in pride of place. MAURA is reading newspapers. Enter MAY from bedroom, dressed for going out.]

MAY — I'm running down to the supermarket.

[Cheerfully and for MAURA'S ears only:]

I'll be glad when that man gets back to work! He's insatiable.

MAURA — I take it he's out of danger then....

MAY — And what about me?

MAURA — There's another photo in the Guardian

MAY — Mmmm... Takes a good picture, doesn't he.... I see they've arrested four people up in Kilburn,,,, Any names?

MAURA — They're holding them under the PTA

MAY — The what?

LUKE — (Off) Prevention of Terrorism Act. The police can hold them for forty-eight hours without charging them.... seven days if they get an order from the Secretary of State

MAY Is that Michael?

LUKE (Off) It was

MAY ....

LUKE (Off) They won't give names unless they charge them

MAY Shan't be long

[Exit MAY.]

LUKE (Off) May!

[Enter LUKE, zipping up his fly. His head is now only lightly bandaged.]

Where is she?

MAURA Shops.
How is the head?

LUKE Itchy. That's a good sign, isn't it?

MAURA Healing
You've seen the papers?
The Guardian says they've already offered you Haverton's seat.

LUKE No thanks.
How are you, Maura?

MAURA Aggggh........... I'd love to get away to the sun for a couple of weeks...........

LUKE — I can let you have some money

MAURA — ....
You're a very generous man, Luke
No. I have enough, thank you......

LUKE — I'd go with you at the drop of a............ bandage! Ha ha ha ha (His bandage is slipping)

MAURA — I'll do it.
Sit down.

[MAURA will carefully and gently fix the bandage,]

What about your big shares case?

LUKE — They've adjourned it for fourteen days.... because of this. I am actually free to go....

MAURA — May would love to go away with you for a few days.....

LUKE — If that's what you wish

MAURA — ....
I'd like to go away on my own. I need it

LUKE — I need people: a woman, particularly
....
I feel very close to you, Maura

MAURA — You are very close to me

[She moves a bit away.]

LUKE — It's more than just......... physical

MAURA	That's the old dualist fallacy: you should know better
LUKE	I mean it's more than just lust
MAURA	Lust covers a multitude of virtues! I've been reading Reich
LUKE	Reich?
MAURA	He's a kind of SuperFreud: reckons all neuroses can be cured by a good fuck
LUKE	Oh I'm a convinced Reichian: maybe you didn't know that, Maura. I've been preaching Reich all my life!
MAURA	He died in prison in the U.S. of A. .... A cot death in the cradle of free speech.......
LUKE	.... You're a very angry young woman
MAURA	About certain things, yes
LUKE	A funny mixture of................. Maura.......... Since the shooting, you've been really kind to me......... loving, I might almost say. But................
MAURA	Go on. 'But.....'
LUKE	I've been listening very carefully: you haven't said one word of............ condemnation

MAURA Whom should I condemn?

LUKE Terrorists. Murderers

MAURA ……………………………………………
One man's terrorist is………. (another man's freedom-fighter.)

LUKE The IRA simply doesn't understand the British mind

MAURA Ah! The unfathomable British mind……. Poor Mau Mau, ZAPU, Makarios, Nasser, Aden, Malaya…….. if only they understood the inscrutable colonial mind….

LUKE That's all history: the reality of today is that we want nothing for Ireland but peace, prosperity and yes, independence. Dignity. We've grown up. Ireland has to grow up too. It's not Britain any more…..

MAURA You know, my father, Bill, is convinced that he and May were made for each other, if she'd only grow up. He has the most romantic feelings for her. Even now, he can't understand why she left him.
……………………………………
May tells me that in the……… what? fifteen years or something, she lived with him as his wife, he raped her repeatedly….. relentlessly, dutifully, as only a good Catholic Irish husband could…..

LUKE A rather crude analogy

MAURA .... It's all so complicated when you love them both........... Well. I love him anyway; he gave me so much attention. May has no time for kids.

....

I'm just remembering the day she finally left......... Bill weeping in incomprehension. She told him she had to go before she did something terrible. Can you imagine poor May doing something terrible?

....

So, I decided to stay with good old Bill, the rapist! .... I need Bill more than I need May.
That's my story. Ha! One of my stories

LUKE Tell me another story

MAURA I didn't come over, all the way from Dublin, just to exchange clichés with the .... Lion of the Inner Temple! Is that what they call it?

LUKE What did you come over for?

MAURA ....?
To see my dear mother and my brother

LUKE Me?

MAURA You did cross my mind

LUKE In what context?

MAURA ....

LUKE May might be perfectly happy to see us paired off

MAURA Women don't see relationships simply in terms of sex

LUKE We all know what she's been through

MAURA Have you ever been raped?

LUKE Of course not

MAURA Me neither

LUKE Well, uh……… I don't know, maybe I was……. in boarding school………. I was only ten, maybe eleven……….. (Shudders)

MAURA I didn't mean to…………………

LUKE I'm a bit thick-skinned. I got over it

MAURA ………………… Maybe men can handle these things better………..

LUKE ………………………
May's not frigid, y'know. Just……………..

MAURA A little problem coming under starter's orders eh?

LUKE Ha! A wee bit shy getting into the box! Ha

MAURA Ha ha ha! A terror over the jumps, what!

LUKE And on the flat! Ha ha ha!

MAURA ……………………………….
I don't think you really have much to worry about, Luke. Just don't use the whip and spurs………

LUKE — There is a quality in doing things with May........ even mundane things, that makes me feel really alive

MAURA — You're not very loyal to her

LUKE — I would be if she let me in................ a proper husband. I am capable of a great deal of love, Maura. It was meeting May t.......

MAURA — You met on a train..........

LUKE — No. In some godforsaken racecourse down in...........

MAURA — Goodwood

LUKE — Goodwood? You could be right

MAURA — I know my history: it's a family trait

LUKE — ....
I think you like to be a bit of a mystery woman

MAURA — I'm boring. I mean, socially. None of the popular neuroses. The only psychologist I know comes to me with his problems: he's always in a mess

LUKE — If you gave me a statement like that in Court, I'd say you're lying

MAURA — We're not in Court, first of all: and secondly, I'm not lying. I hate lies!

LUKE

I have the distinct feeling we're not talking enough about things that need to be said between us. That may be my fault. If we don't discuss how we feel, while we have the chance........

MAURA

You keep trying to make something out of nothing, Luke

LUKE

It's not nothing. I know about gut feeling: I make a very good living from them.

MAURA

....
If there's something going on between us, it may not be very pleasant

LUKE

There's a lot of fear......... or anger or........ passion: I don't pretend to be able to tell....... All down around the tail stump. Not very civilized, is it?

MAURA

We're only animals..........

LUKE

That doesn't frighten me

MAURA

...........Except we have a soul......... and a God

LUKE

A God would be nice............ Even a soul

MAURA

I suspected you were a pagan

LUKE

A lapsed pagan. I used to be a lapsed C. of E., but I lost the faith! Ha ha ha!

MAURA

Religion is very important to me....... It ties things up.......... Makes sense of it all

LUKE

Mmm A delicious luxury!

MAURA — You can afford it

LUKE — ....

Does it all really make sense to you, Maura?

MAURA — Yes

LUKE — Beep! Sorry: my Lie Detector keeps going off at the inappropriate moment................ ....

You're like a .... Have you ever seen one of those really big rat traps? They'd take your finger off if they went off.............

MAURA — Yes, I've used them

LUKE — Are people quite........ tense over there with all the...........

MAURA — Tense? God!
You want to see the sheer apathy in its natural habitat, just come over to Dublin for a weekend!
The Irish people........... Did you ever see a man trying to push a car with a little rope?

LUKE — Pull

MAURA — I'm talking about Ireland. Push

LUKE — Ha ha ha! And the Car is................ ?

MAURA — Never mind

LUKE — If we all turned round and went the other way, we could pull it

MAURA You may just have solved the Anglo-Irish problem, Luke. Wouldn't it be just like you!

LUKE I never used to talk politics.......... People are much more interesting. I mean, personal things. Relationships...........

MAURA Too dangerous

LUKE .... And you can do something about them!

MAURA ....

[Enter TOM, with carrier-bags of groceries.]

TOM May caught me trying to slip past her on the Portobello Road.....

LUKE Where is she?

TOM Last I saw of her, she was plunging fearlessly in among the fruit-stalls

LUKE I'll go down and rescue her. If we miss each other, tell her I'll be in The Swan. Anyone for a wee *aperitif* ?

TOM Not just now

MAURA Too early for me

LUKE You're very badly brought up, the pair of you: "The daylight hours are the hours for drinking....."
That's Dr Johnson, in case you don't know

MAURA Any winners today, Luke?

LUKE Come down to The Swan about 1.30 and I'll make your fortune for you. I have to phone a man at one.

……………………………………

You were to phone me at The Savoy on the day I…. Did you do it?

MAURA I tried. It was engaged

LUKE Of course.

……………………………

Well, The Swan about half past one. See you then my dears….
Maura, I'd like…………………

TOM Cheers

[Exit Luke.]

MAURA <u>Slán</u>

TOM Jesus! "<u>Slán</u>"

MAURA Have you some objection?

TOM Not if you're an Irish speaker

MAURA It's a start

TOM …………………………

Who is 'George'?

MAURA Sorry?

TOM A bloke called George phoned last night

MAURA Any message?

TOM	No Who is he?
MAURA	Met him on the plane
TOM	He didn't sound like a 'George' to me: he had a Kerry accent as thick as a pound of butter
MAURA	So much for stereotyping
TOM	.... Nobody claimed the murder yet
MAURA	....
TOM	MAURA!
MAURA	So it's murder now
TOM	Of course
MAURA	You've come a long way
TOM	.... Anyone we know picked up?
MAURA	....
TOM	Have I said something wrong?
MAURA	I don't know any murderers
TOM	.... Bill told me in a letter, you've left the Workers' Party............ He seemed quite chuffed about it

MAURA So was I

TOM Socialism is the only thing he fears more than Hell

MAURA For such a great Revolutionary Thinker, you seem to have little faith in the possibility of a man changing

....

You had no right to leave, Tom. Their private problem was none of your business

TOM May was ready for a mental home. So was I. We should have insisted you come with us....

MAURA You did your damnedest.
Bill blames you, to a great extent, for breaking up their marriage. You opposed him at every turn....

TOM I should think I did, I....

MAURA I remember myself: you and May... always exclusive..... secretive. You gave him nothing

TOM Seventeen years.
You ask May what that was like, as a wife

MAURA She was never a wife to him: you know she has sexual problems

TOM — She has now.
Well, ask me what it was like, having that drunken slob as a father, since I was that high.... Doing his utmost to push me into the Provisional-mad-bloody-bomber-brigade, and of course.....

MAURA — You don't have the slightest idea what you're talking about!

TOM — .... And of course making bloody sure he stayed safely on the ditch himself

MAURA — It's a pity you never bothered getting to know the man

TOM — ....
If he's conned you into anything, I'll........

MAURA — Like you conned me into the Official IRA, is it?

TOM — Never! I never suggested or encouraged you in any one way t..........

MAURA — Take responsibility for your actions, for once in your life!

TOM — I was out of........... everything, before you ever dreamt of joining

MAURA — ....
From when I was about twelve or thirteen, I had this recurring dream....

TOM — I'm not taking responsibility for your dreams

MAURA — I must have had it about twenty or thirty times.
I'm climbing the steps of this high tower with you and we have some sort of big gun, like a rocket-launcher or something and I have to carry it though it's nearly as big as me, 'cos you're wounded and only you can fire it and we only had two minutes to destroy this bridge that the Brits would be crossing to engulf us, and if we didn't pull it off it would be the end of everything

TOM — I have no stomach for violence

MAURA — That's a new one

TOM — There was no call for you to go shoving your arm in the fire when I was already running clear of it........
No sense

MAURA — You never told me you quit

TOM — I never told you I joined: I didn't announce it in the Social and Personal Columns

MAURA — Bill said you were over here on an operation: as a sleeper

TOM — For Christsake: Bill!

MAURA — It hung together. I mean, I never knew anyone just upped and walked away from the Official IRA

TOM — I'd done my bit......

MAURA — So had I

TOM — I wished you had talked to me before you joined

MAURA — I did: a thousand times
Anyway, they tried to shoot me when I quit

TOM — Jesus
....
Were you leaving to join some other.... military outfit?

MAURA — ....

TOM — Did you try to take any Army gear with you?

MAURA — ....

TOM — You see. My case was different.
....
I was getting out of politics for keeps

MAURA — You're in the Labour party here

TOM — That doesn't count as politics!

[They BOTH laugh a little.
Enter MAY from buying fruit and vegetables.]

MAY — It's lovely to see the two of you together again

TOM — Ecstatic!

MAY — I don't know how we get through all the food in this house. I'm not doing another pennyworth of shopping this week: I don't care if you all starve

TOM — What's cheap out there today?

MAY — I got a nice cauliflower for forty pence: two pineapples for a pound

MAURA — Well done

TOM — They're usually top price on Saturdays

MAURA — I'll put them away for you

TOM — Did Luke find you?

[Exit MAY and MAURA to Kitchen. TOM sits with head in his hands.]

MAY — (Off) No

MAURA — (Off) He'll be in the pub

MAY — I'll just wash my hands and............

[Enter MAY.]

Are you all right?

TOM — I was just thinking......... about Dublin

MAY — I'll make you a cup of coffee

TOM — ....

Does Luke know about........ my politics?

MAY — Not from me.

You've told him often enough you're a

Communist: I don't think he believes you

TOM I wonder am I..... y'know, in their files over here: the Special Branch

MAY I wouldn't think so, Tom. They'd have been round to see you after one of the bombings if you were.... They must have covered everyone after Brighton.... Harrods.... all those

TOM ....
....
For the first time in seven years, I feel I'm here under false pretences

MAY You've put those seven years' hard work into this country: that's how the Englishman judges you. You owe him nothing

TOM And what do I owe the Irishman?

MAY What did we ever get from Ireland only poverty and .... oppression and resentment and, and........ history!

TOM History is good for you, once you don't swallow it without chewing

MAY ....Ah, that's not true either: I got a lot of innocent fun and friendship in Ireland... and the love of music..... when I was young...
Over here, the children have no innocence: everything happens too soon for them. In Ireland you can be a child till you're....

TOM — The problem in Ireland starts when you try to grow up

MAY — Oh yes: it's no place for an adult

TOM — Tír Na nÓg! (The ancient idea of Paradise was the Land Of Ever-Young.) The Republic of Ireland is our self-fulfilled prophecy

MAY — Ireland, y'see, can't grow up till the British get out

TOM — But the Brits, y'see, can't get out till the Irish grow up

MAY — Or till the British grow up

TOM — And get out

[They laugh a little.]

MAY — This violence is..... infantile

TOM — But deadly serious: like religion.... and football

MAY — Everyone needs something to believe in.

....

I believe in...... I love old things. Old clocks..... old people...... old ways.....old songs

TOM — We have to write some new songs

MAY — You hate my sentimentality and my..... dependence. For a woman, dependence was the reality in our culture

TOM	You behave as if you came out of the nineteenth century
MAY	I never felt part of this
TOM	Well you are. Use your memories..... to construct a vision
MAY	You have the education. It's too late for me to think about visions
TOM	<u>Don't say that!</u>
MAY	.... I expect you'd be happy if I had a job
TOM	Don't spend your whole life trying to please people
MAY	I like pleasing people
TOM	Being pleased doesn't please me!
MAY	You want me to be something that doesn't make you uncomfortable .... I'll do something for myself: don't be angry
TOM	I'll be angry if I want to be
MAY	You sound like my father
TOM	I feel like your father. Bringing up parents is a terrible responsibility these days
MAY	....

I'm just remembering your temper as a little boy.........

TOM Maura had the temper

MAY Only about twice.
Once, outside the cinema on O'Connell Street.... I can still see the vicious little red face of you: I wouldn't take you in to see Snow White for the umpteenth time: I was thoroughly sick of Snow White: you lay down on the footpath and kicked and screamed like a lunatic for about half an hour: you said, 'I hate you and I wish you were dead!'

TOM Never

MAY You did. You said, 'And you're the worst mother I ever had!'

TOM You're the best mother I ever had

MAY I suppose I wasn't too bad

TOM ....
If I went home for a year or two.....

MAY This is your home

TOM We should have insisted Maura came with us

MAY He said he'd fight for her to the highest court in the land..... Her religion was all he was worried about. He's written the two of us off as lost souls!

TOM	He's a procurer for the whore-house of Catholic Nationalism. He pretended to Maura that I was over here on some long-term mission.... A sleeper
MAY	Sleeper?
TOM	What is Maura here for?
MAY	You don't have to ask why anyone wants to get away from Bill
TOM	She won't hear a word against him
MAY	I'm so glad to have the two of you here with me, I.....
TOM	Ask her to stay
MAY	A nice young man rang several times from Ireland
TOM	With a Kerry accent?
MAY	George. They're going to share a flat or something
TOM	She told me she met him on the plane......
MAY	I met Luke on a train
TOM	Just a few days ago
MAY	Ah no: it's been going on for over a year. George rang this morning: he just phoned to say he'd got home safely from some business trip..... he seemed really anxious to have her back

TOM What business is he in?

MAY I've no idea

TOM Maura used to tell me everything

MAY You've changed here: I'm not criticising you, but...... in Ireland your critical faculties were directed against the political system sort of thing. Now you criticise people personally..... how they live. That's not so easy to take

TOM ....

MAY Like your campaign to get me out to work

TOM There was no campaign

MAY You actually put me off change: put me on the defensive. You don't give people credit for any intelligence

TOM I'm impatient

MAY The effect can be reactionary

....

....

....

Actually..... I was offered a job last week: just down the road. The funny Architect man that drinks Pernod with sugar and lemonade in The Swan.... He needs a kind of Office Manager

TOM A kinder Office Manager is what you'd be, May! The very kindest

MAY	If he's in the pub today, I was going to tell him I'll give it a whirl
TOM	Great
MAY	I'm not doing it to please you. .... For your information, I had also made up my mind months ago, to divorce Bill as soon as I got a job. I wrote him a long letter telling him how good it'd be for both of us
TOM	You never told me that
MAY	Because I didn't post it. I still have it in my room. I hadn't finally made up my mind. I mean everything I said to you is true. It suits all of us for me to be dependent. Who's going to iron the shirts? I shan't have time
TOM	We'll take turns. I do my share of the cooking
MAY	Because you enjoy it
Tom	I'll do it
MAY	There's a basket full of clothes in the hot cupboard
TOM	I'll do them tonight
MAY	I'll believe it when I see it .... It's mostly my old bras.... And pants
TOM	....

You don't need to iron........ those things

MAY I do. I hate the feel of clothes that haven't been pressed

TOM ....
Maybe the job will be gone before you meet him. Anyway, I'm not sure I want my mother working for a man who drinks Pernod with sugar and lemonade: it sounds like a dangerous affectation to me!

MAY You don't want me to liberate myself, Tom: you just want me as someone to preach at

TOM Shush! I think I've just invented disposable women's underwear

MAY And men's

[Enter MAURA; searching]

TOM Men don't go around asking for starched Y-fronts

MAY There's a clever answer to that, but I can't think of it

MAURA Anyone see my handbag?

MAY Who's coming down to the Swan?

MAURA You two go

TOM Not me.
Will I do a cauliflower-cheese for lunch?

MAY That'd be delicious.
See you sweethearts!

[Exit MAY]

MAURA — *Slán*

………….

You needn't roll your eyes

[MAURA is looking for her bag.]

TOM — I said nothing

MAURA — Are you sitting on my bag?

TOM — Probably

MAURA — Would you mind shifting yourself and see….

[TOM feels around behind him: he freezes as he identifies something familiar in MAURA'S handbag.]

TOM — No

MAURA — ……………………..?

I could have sworn I…..

TOM — ……………………….

Maura………

MAURA — Get up for a second

TOM — Maura….. in Dublin, in the attic…. I had a really clever little arms dump in the brickwork of th…..

[MAURA dives at TOM'S chair. They struggle: she comes up with the handbag, but its contents spill on TOM'S lap, including a .38 revolver. TOM scrambles to his feet with the gun, managing to hold MAURA off.]

TOM — Hah.... I.... I... just felt something familiar.... Amazing! I recognised it... my old .38.....

MAURA — You lost any right to it when you ran away

TOM — Says who? Says who?

MAURA — Says me: and says the Provisional IRA. Give it here!

TOM — Oh it's the Provos, is it? I thought more of you.... Thought you might have gone for something with some semblance of real politics.....

MAURA — You know nothing about real politics: you're out of date*!* *Passé!*

TOM — I'm going to dump this in the Thames

MAURA — I'll fucking dump you in the Thames!

TOM — You've sunk very low

MAURA — You can't face up to your own failure: as an Irishman, as a revolutionary... as a man! And you can't face up to me, a woman and your own sister, doing what you haven't the guts for....

TOM — I've faced my own attitude to violence, if that's what you mean. I said it before, I've no stomach for violence.

That's not failure: it's good.... It's a step forward

MAURA — You're using violence now.... controlling me with that gun

TOM — It's my gun. I want my gun out of Irish politics. I'm forced to react to your commitment to violence

MAURA — With a gun. That's the argument for a just war. It's the argument for resistance in arms to the Brits in Ireland

[TOM and MAURA are almost imperceptibly circling for advantage.]

TOM — I'm going out to throw my gun in the Thames. This is unilateral disarmament...

MAURA — I'm taking the .38

TOM — I'm probably stronger

MAURA — I'm stronger.
Give

TOM — I won't give

MAURA — All I'm asking is the freedom to make my own choices

TOM — I've been happy in this city... probably happier than I've ever been in my life.
I feel an obligation to protect it from...

MAURA You're protecting your own hide: nothing else

TOM I've had more freedom, more support, more opportunity to be what I want to be, here than I ever got or ever looked like getting in the so called free part of my own country: that gives me food for thought

MAURA You didn't have to come here to know that England was always ready to give that sort of freedom to any Irishman that played the Imperialist game for them... from Castlereagh...... Oscar Wilde..... Shaw down to..... Terry fucking Wogan. Nothing they like better than an Irish clown or two around the place

TOM I'm not playing the Imperialist game or the clown: I'm trying to renew myself and....

MAURA Jaysus

TOM ...... And help Britain and Ireland to renew themselves

MAURA The only way Britain renews itself is in blood

TOM And holy Ireland?

MAURA Yes.
Until the connection is broken.
Yeats knew that. Pearse knew it

TOM Pair of fascists

MAURA Connolly knew it

TOM Stupid. His duty was to keep himself alive: there was no one else. Labour has never recovered from it

MAURA He knew. Independence is the *sine qua non* for Irish politics

TOM If it was true in 1916, which I doubt, it certainly isn't true now. You saw what came out of the woodwork in Ireland during the Abortion referendum.... God!

MAURA I'm against abortion

TOM I wouldn't doubt you: it cuts down the numbers available for butchery later on

MAURA ....
It seems we don't agree on much any more

TOM ....
....
Why are you in London?

MAURA Family visit. I'm very attached....
to my mother

TOM ....
....
If you were involved in the Haverton murder, I'll.....

MAURA Oh you'd be the very first to know if I did! I mean, you are my big brother: your wonderful Stalinist friends taught me how to kill....

TOM .... I'll turn you in; I swear it!

MAURA One of these days you're going to surprise me. I suppose informing is now Official IRA policy. Sorry, there is no Official IRA, is there? Workers' Party policy

TOM ....
I'm trying to believe it's not possible.... That you could share this, your mother's house.... her table... drink the health of ... flirt with... the man who but for a hairsbreadth... whose best friend was gunned down in his arms.... I saw Luke embracing you with those arms.... in which our mother sleeps in love.....

MAURA Aw shut your drivelling mouth, Tom!

TOM I can't believe in you

[TOM starts to raise the revolver.]

MAURA Put down that gun

TOM You should be put down like a mad dog

[Unheard, LUKE and MAY have come back and stand in the doorway. LUKE carries a bottle of wine. MAURA sees them.]

MAURA PUT THAT GUN DOWN, TOM, OR I'LL PHONE THE POLICE!

MAY TOM!

[MAY rushes straight to TOM and throws herself at his knees in supplication.
LUKE goes gallantly to protect MAURA: stands between them.]

LUKE TOM!

MAY Stop it Tom, for God's sake !

TOM Hello, Luke. I see you've brought some good cheer home with you, as usual. Any winners, Luke? Did you get any winners for our Maura?

LUKE Are you all right, Maura ? Tom?

TOM As can be expected, in the circumstances

LUKE Where the hell did the gun come from ?

TOM Now that's a long story, Luke...

LUKE Is it his, May ?

MAY I... I don't know

LUKE Maura ?

TOM Yes, it's mine

LUKE Is it legal ?

TOM ....
Not in the English sense

LUKE Christ !
....
Do you know anything about this, May?

MAY

Luke.... I've seen guns coming and going in our house all my life. I don't know about them: I don't want to know about them, but they were there and all I knew was to keep my mouth shut about them.
I'll only say this: I've never seen a gun since I left Ireland until this minute, and that's seven years. And wish to God I hadn't seen this one. Tom: I thought............

LUKE

Do you know anything about it, Maura ?

MAURA

....

[MAURA turns away.]

TOM

I was going to throw it in the Thames

LUKE

You were threatening Maura with it

MAY

He wouldn't

TOM

We here having a little argument... about Yeats
Right, Maura ?

MAURA

....

TOM

A deadly serious business, this poetry:

"Out of Ireland have we come.
Great hatred, little room,
Maimed us at the start.
Eh........."

MAURA

".... I carry from my mother's womb
A fanatic heart."

MAY Not mine

[TOM pockets the gun.]

TOM It's all so bloody boring: our age is slipping away in decades of barren violence. There's no growth, Luke. Why don't you clean up the shit you've crapped in my country and let us grow up?

LUKE Why can't you live together like human beings?

TOM ....?
Ha ha ha ha !
I had this image there, of the father cuckoo laying down the Law to the complaining blackbirds

LUKE Serve you right if we pulled out and let you tear each other apart

TOM Quoth the cuckoo !
....
Maybe.... in natural justice, your young cuckoo has the right to lord it over the blackbirds

MAURA Our cuckoos have their own nest to go back to, if they can't stomach being Irish

TOM I can't stomach being Irish: maybe there's too much of the cuckoo in me

MAURA That's not cuckoo: that's canary

TOM *Touché*
....
I must to my river

MAURA — I'll go with you

TOM — Thank you, no

LUKE — I think I need to know more about that weapon, before you do anything. I feel the strongest need for the advice of a good lawyer

TOM — You're the best lawyer I know

LUKE — A good policeman then.
I must, by all the standards I believe in, report what I've seen here today, May

MAY — ……………………
I'll speak to no policeman about my son, Luke !

LUKE — Maura ?

MAURA — It's out of the question

LUKE — You're my…. my family !

MAY — Exactly

LUKE — Any civilized society must be governed by laws

MAURA — Every child knows the answer to that kind of argument, Luke. 'Misgoverning rulers do not command allegiance.' I'm weary of rhetoric….

LUKE — I assume you haven't forgotten what I've been through this week: that wasn't rhetoric: Michael Haverton wasn't done to death by rhetoric

MAURA Are you accusing Tom of being involved in.... ?

MAY Of course not

LUKE I don't know how many Irish people go around London with guns in their pockets ! I mean, is this the norm ? You tell me !

TOM You happen to have witnessed the moment when I decided to take my gun out of Irish politics... for keeps. It was a one-off occurrence

MAY It seems like a good idea, Luke

LUKE Nobody's denying that: but it does beg several questions. Like 'why now?'
Is it because its work is done ? I'd just like to know

MAY ....
.... I've been thinking about my attitude to Bill.... and you, Luke....

LUKE Do you mind if I pursue this matter ?

MAY I decided to divorce your father, Maura

LUKE (To Tom) Why now ?

MAURA You know he won't recognise it ? He's said that a hundred times

TOM Because I'm ready

MAY	Well, he can stay married to me if he likes: I shan't be married to him
LUKE	If that's a proposal May, I wish you'd wait till....
MAY	It's not a proposal
LUKE	You all thrive on chaos ! I'm not getting involved in any firearms conspiracy for you or anyone else, Tom !
MAY	No more marriages for me, thank you
LUKE	Tom...
MAY	I'll go and post that letter to Bill before I change my mind
TOM	The eldest son makes the speech at the Divorce Breakfast y'know ! Who'll give Bill away ?
MAY	Me
LUKE	Tom... frankly, I'd like to have a forensic test done on that .38.... just for the record. It is a .38, isn't it ?
TOM	That might be embarrassing
LUKE	.........................? Christ Almighty !
Tom	I'm talking about when I was a kid... seven or eight years back.... in Ireland
MAY	He's been out of everything for years, Luke

[Exit MAY]

LUKE So how come you bring this gun to England?

TOM ....
....

LUKE How come you didn't throw it in the Liffey?
Is the Liffey so full of guns it won't take any more... ?

TOM I could... at that time.... visualise a situation where I might take up the gun again. That is no longer the case

LUKE So you've been keeping this weapon on ice till you make up your mind whether to use it or no

TOM ....

LUKE Why is it loaded?

TOM Is it ?

LUKE A trained man doesn't store a loaded gun

TOM It's a way of getting rid of the ammo at the same time

LUKE ....
I can hand this gun in to the police 'from a client'... I'm prepared to maintain complete confidentiality, provided it hasn't been used in any crime...

TOM — I told you; there were jobs done with it in Ireland, eight years ago

LUKE — Has it killed anyone ?

TOM — Not that I know of

LUKE — All right... provided there's no connection with crime in the past seven years

TOM — ....

LUKE — You don't trust me

TOM — I do, but......
If it's been used since then, it wasn't with my knowledge....

LUKE — If someone goes off with my gun and sticks up a bank, that's his problem

TOM — I'll not lead the police to any man's door: not if there's politics involved.... not if I support the politics

LUKE — ....
I can't figure you out.
....
....
What do you feel about the murder of Michael Haverton ?

TOM — ....

LUKE — I mean.... What about the man who shot me in the head ?

TOM — ....

	Obviously, you weren't intended as the victim...
LUKE	So, to some extent at least, you support them killing Michael
TOM	I don't support them
LUKE	Well... 'sympathise'... or or 'understand' them in some w....
TOM	I think I understand them. I don't support or sympathise with them. They are anathema to me, politically... But there is a niggling voice, somewhere... back there.... saying theirs may be the only way......
LUKE	But the public fact is, all the Irish have to do is stop fighting among thems.....
TOM	Hark ! The cuckoo is back
MAURA	You sent the Loyalist settlers over there t....
LUKE	I didn't send anyone anywhere, Maura, love
MAURA	You... England.... Britain, sent them to wipe the native Irish off the map. They failed. Call them back, or let them accept Irish nationality. Their mission failed
LUKE	.... It seems to me that the rather unpalatable fact for you, is.... they didn't fail. The settlers won. They secured Ulster, if not Ireland, for the Crown... yes, by force of arms, because that's how

things were done in those days. And the Crown has held Ulster securely ever since...

TOM — 'Held' is the problem, isn't it ?
Never quite won...

MAURA — Resisted in arms by the native Irish in every generation. The game is not over, Luke

LUKE — A pipe-dream. The whistle blew in 1690

TOM — We're a bit hard of hearing over there, Luke..... if they did hear a whistle, they reckon we've gone into extra time !

LUKE — Ah no: King William 3... King James 0 ! Ha ha ha ha !

TOM — That only settled the Calcutta Cup for 1690... the Triple Crown remains undecided! Ha ha ha ha!

[MAURA explodes.]

MAURA — <u>The pair of you can laugh and joke about it all you like... but there's people dying on the streets of Belfast and Derry...</u>

LUKE — <u>There are people dying on the streets of London, Maura.</u>
Half an inch the other way and my admittedly inadequate brains would have been plastered all over the Savoy Grill with Michael Haverton's: I'm laughing because I'm alive to laugh and please don't try to take that away from me !

[MAURA collapses.]

MAURA ....
SICK OF IT ! I'M SICK OF TALK !

[MAURA is shaking.]

LUKE ....

[LUKE goes to put his arms around her: MAURA jerks nervously out of his way.]

I'm sorry

MAURA Leave me be

LUKE ....
A few days ago, I think I could safely say I was the happiest man in... well, I was really happy
....
....
I look on you as my own son,,,, my own daughter.... my wife, May...

TOM But we're not. We're Bill's. Big Bill the racist rapist's family. I'm his son... Maura his daughter... May, his wife, I believe you've met

LUKE That's cruel

TOM I'm trying to be realistic

LUKE I love each one of you

TOM I love you, Luke... but not like a father, if you don't mind. It has unpleasant connotations for me. Maura there understands a father's little problems better than I

MAURA At least Bill has some principles... morals

TOM Our Maura has the Holy Grail hid in her knickers y'know... a wee present Bill brought back from a day-excursion to Newry

LUKE I never think much about morals. I live by the Law of the land, more or less... and some kind of residual Christian morality where the law is obviously 'a ass'....

MAURA A few hours back you wanted to ditch May and hustle me off to a Greek island or something. What kind of morality is that ?

LUKE I don't know what you two are trying to do to me, but it's very unpleasant to be on the receiving end of it

....

Am I supposed to feel guilty for getting in the way of an IRA murder squad, or for coming home before I'm expected and finding the pair of you playing Rambo round the living room with that phallic transitional object of yours ?

....

....

As for our conversation this morning, Maura, I really think you might have treated that with some discretion.........

TOM Ah discretion: have I e'er offended thee ?

LUKE ...... As Tom says, the reality is, you're not my daughter....

TOM Yessum: the man is right

LUKE May is not my wife. I'm a free man and you're a free woman...

TOM Hallelujah

[Enter MAY with her letter for Bill.]

MAURA TOM, WOULD YOU SHUT YOUR BLOODY FACE FOR GODSAKE!

TOM Yessum I w...

MAURA DECADENT ! THAT'S WHAT YOU ARE ! BOTH OF YOU ! DECADENT ! THIS COUNTRY STINKS LIKE A HUGE ROTTEN COLONIAL CORPSE !
Christ ! I can't breathe.....

[Shaking, MAURA tries to use the phone, but can't handle it.]

May, find Aer Lingus for me

[MAY knows the number.]

MAY 734 1212

MAURA Dial it for me

[MAY dials it and hands the phone to MAURA.]

MAURA Hello.... Can I get on a flight to Dublin today ? ......Are you sure ? .... What about stand-by ? .... Shit !

[She hangs up]

I'll go by boat.
Sorry May, I... can't stand it here: I have to get back home !

TOM Are you going by Holyhead ?

MAURA Yes, I suppose so

TOM ....
I'll travel with you if you like

MAY Tom !

TOM I'm going back, May. We haven't the right to leave it to the Mauras and the Bills....

MAURA Oh Tom !

[MAURA would hug him.]

And I can get that .38 through the Customs, no bother !

TOM I have to tell you, Maura.... I'm going back to fight you and everything you stand for. There's a smell of rotting corpses here all right and it came in with you. I don't know if it can be washed out of it, ever

MAURA Don't waste your money coming back to my country

TOM 'Your country !'

MAURA Stay here and play Pagliacci for them: they'll look after you

[TOM hands LUKE the gun.]

TOM You decide what to do with that

MAURA Put one foot in Ireland and you're dead meat !

MAY Don't say that, child !

LUKE I wish you'd both stay: we need time...

MAY For God's sake stay, Maura

MAURA Give us that gun, Luke: keep the ammunition if you want.... I.....

LUKE You have the Customs squared, no problem..... ?

....

....

MAURA Yes

LUKE ....

It was you brought Tom's gun over here..... What did you want him to..... ?

MAURA I promise it'll be out of England tonight

LUKE ...... Why ?

TOM Let's go and pack, Maura....

MAURA Pack yourself away to Hell. Scum !

MAY — Let her go, Tom: Ireland is no place for you..... you've grown up. It's going back, like you said, to the seventeenth century

LUKE — Why, Maura ? Tom didn't want it: you knew that

MAURA — ....

TOM — She knows only history

LUKE — Were you trying to reactivate him as a t.....

MAURA — Tom is dead. I know no Tom

LUKE — ....
Please tell me why you brought a gun to England, Maura

MAURA — I SHIT ON ENGLAND !

LUKE — ....
You..................?
Oh Maura !

MAURA — ....
I......... I came over here to set up an ex......
....
....
Michael Haverton was tried in his absence by the Army Council of Oglaigh na hEireann and found guilty of conspiracy to murder and other crimes against the Irish people. He was sentenced to death by assassination....

LUKE — Ah no !

MAURA — The sentence has now been carried out

MAY Jesus !

[MAURA lifts her bag and walks towards the door.]

You're all I have.....
Maura, love, don't say these terrible things.....

MAURA ....
You've left the love and affection bit about twenty years too late, May !

MAY You're all I have or care about... the three of you...

[MAY raises her arms in a gesture of encompassing compassion.]

LUKE Yes

MAY All I love

LUKE All I love

TOM Closer than a family

LUKE Yes

MAY Yes

MAURA My last year in school, Mother Superior said I could be anything I set my mind on............
....
I said, I'd be a teacher.....

[Exit MAURA. The others stare after her in silence. The music

[... rises around them to fill the theatre: the opening lines of THESE FOOLISH THINGS. Hold lights for about six seconds.]

RECORD PLAYS

Oh will you never let me be !
Oh will you never set me free !
The ties that bound us, are still around us......

[Fade to BLACKOUT as music continues.]

END

www.ingramcontent.com/pod-product-compliance
Ingram Content Group UK Ltd.
Pitfield, Milton Keynes, MK11 3LW, UK
UKHW020201200726
13856UKWH00003B/1133